JESSIXA BAGLEY AND AARON BAGLEY

VINCENT COMES HOME

A NEAL PORTER BOOK
ROARING BROOK PRESS
NEW YORK

Copyright © 2018 by Jessixa and Aaron Bagley

A Neal Porter Book

Published by Roaring Brook Press

Roaring Brook Press is a division of Holtzbrinck Publishing Holdings Limited Partnership

175 Fifth Avenue, New York, NY 10010

mackids.com

The art for this book was created using pen and watercolor.

Library of Congress Control Number: 2017944679

ISBN: 978-1-62672-780-9

Our books may be purchased in bulk for promotional, educational, or business use. Please
contact your local bookseller or the Macmillan Corporate and Premium Sales Department
at (800) 221-7945 ext. 5442 or by e-mail at MacmillanSpecialMarkets@macmillan.com.

First edition 2018

Book design by Jennifer Browne

Printed in China by RR Donnelley Asia Printing Solutions Ltd., Dongguan City, Guangdong Province

1 3 5 7 9 10 8 6 4 2

For Debbie

Vincent lived on a cargo ship.
His paws had never touched land.

Ship life was good. Fresh fish whenever he wanted. Seagulls to chase all day long.

And the night stars that charted the ship's course were the most beautiful sight he could imagine.

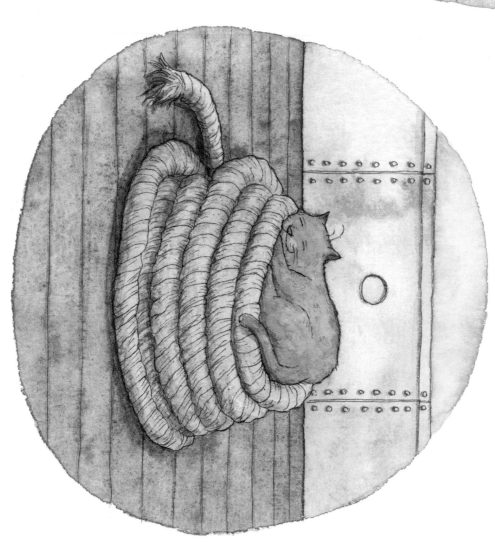

Vincent went about as he pleased.

No one seemed to notice him much.

The *Domus* carried goods from one port to another.

They'd load up with chocolate from Zanzibar and deliver it to Norway, oranges from Florida ended up in Iceland.

Always coming and going.

Never staying.

Vincent loved traveling to exciting new places,
each one different from the last . . .

but he could only enjoy them from a distance.

The captain collected souvenirs from each port they stopped at and displayed them in his cabin, Vincent's favorite place on the ship. They seemed to have visited every place imaginable.

Every place except one.

"Even though we are far away, it's nice to know that home is always there," said the second mate.

"I can't wait to get home," said the first mate.

"The most exotic food in the world can't compare to a home-cooked meal," said the cook. "Whenever I go home, I never want to leave."

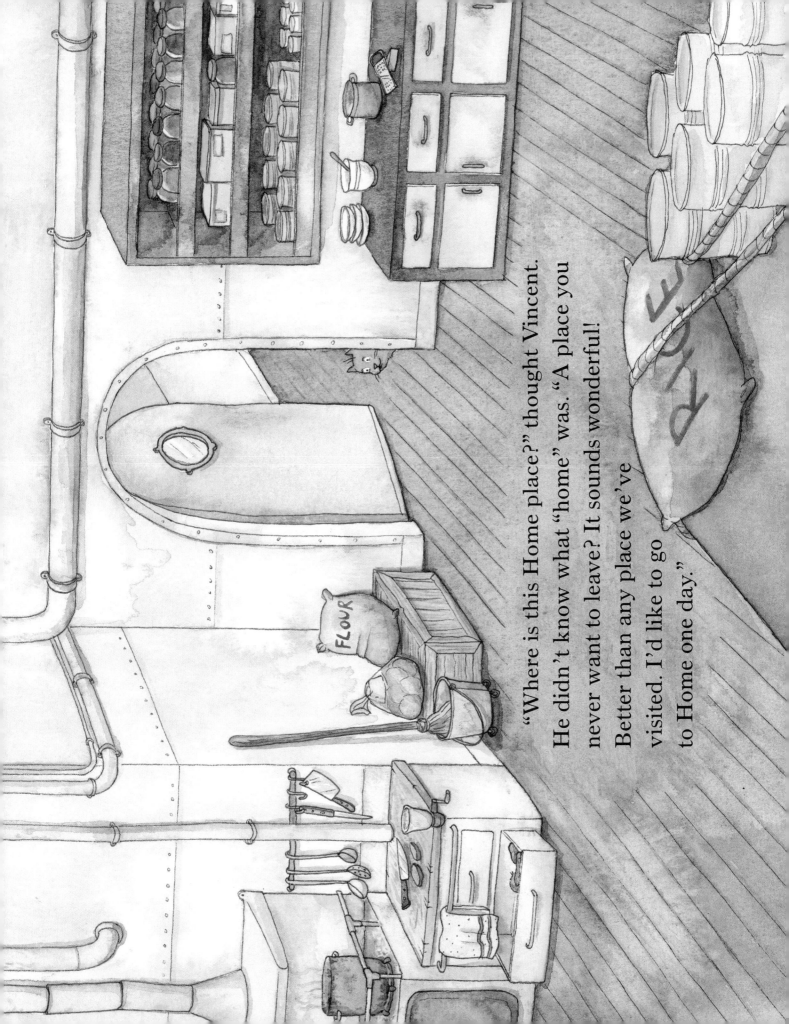

"Where is this Home place?" thought Vincent. He didn't know what "home" was. "A place you never want to leave? It sounds wonderful! Better than any place we've visited. I'd like to go to Home one day."

The next day the ship pulled
into another fine city.
"All hands on deck!"
"Prepare to drop anchor!"

Vincent heard the first mate shout, "We're HOME!!!"

The rest of the crew cheered.

"This is it! We have made it to Home!" thought Vincent. "I can't wait to see it. Home must be the best place in the world!"

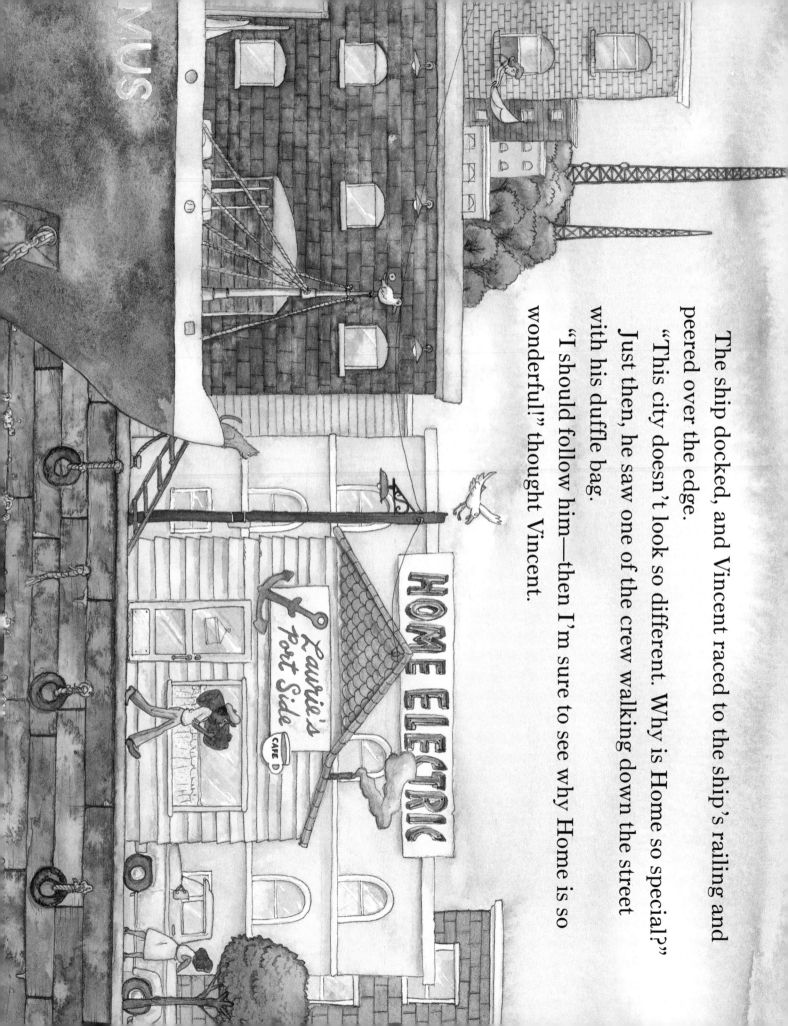

The ship docked, and Vincent raced to the ship's railing and peered over the edge.

"This city doesn't look so different. Why is Home so special?" Just then, he saw one of the crew walking down the street with his duffle bag.

"I should follow him—then I'm sure to see why Home is so wonderful!" thought Vincent.

He followed the crewman for a while, until he got to a building. As the crewman opened the door, a bunch of people yelled "WELCOME HOME!"

Vincent watched as all the people hugged and kissed the crewman. "This is Home?" thought Vincent. "I thought Home was some amazing new city." He watched through the window for a long time as they ate and laughed and laughed and talked together. They all looked so happy.

He left and walked around for a long time.
He looked in a lot of windows and saw similar scenes.
And one thing was the same in all the windows.

"Home isn't just a place," he thought. "Home is where the people who love you are. I guess I don't have a Home."

Vincent padded around and looked up at the quiet night sky. At least the stars would always be there.

Just then he heard a familiar sound.

"There you are, my boy! I've been looking all over for you! You've never left the ship before," said the captain.

The captain scooped him up and scratched him under his chin and rubbed his belly.

"Let's go home."